jE VAISBERG Diego
Dino /
Vaisberg, Diego,

To Simón and Leia, for turning my world upside down
and making every day an adventure

Copyright © 2017 by Diego Vaisberg

First U.S. edition 2018

Library of Congress Catalog Card Number pending
ISBN 978-1-5362-0280-9

18 19 20 21 22 23 WKT 10 9 8 7 6 5 4 3 2 1

Printed in Shenzhen, Guangdong, China

This book was typeset in Brandon Grotesque.
The illustrations were created digitally and printed
in Pantone Warm Red and Pantone 300 (blue).

TEMPLAR BOOKS

an imprint of
Candlewick Press
99 Dover Street
Somerville, Massachusetts 02144
www.candlewick.com

DINO

Diego Vaisberg

templar books
an imprint of Candlewick Press

One day a gigantic egg
appeared in our backyard.

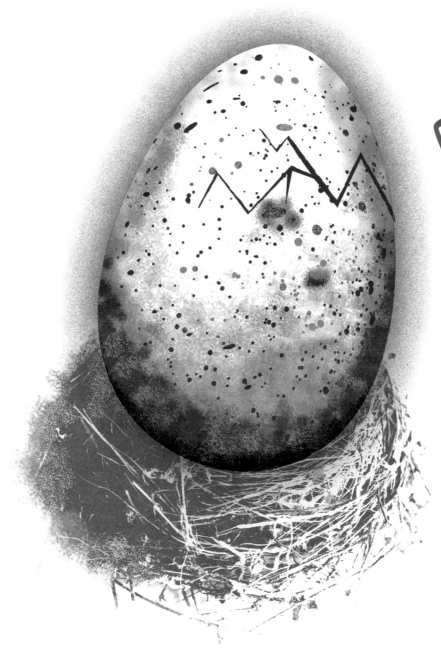

CRACK!

We thought it might be a giant canary . . .

TWEET!
TWEET!

or one of those big lizards that show up
in the summer . . .

or maybe a huge tortoise.

But it wasn't any of those things.

It was a
dinosaur!

He was so cute and friendly
that we decided to keep him.

We named him Dino,
and from that day on,
he was our pet.

Dino wasn't very big at first.

ROAR!

But he grew,

and grew,

and grew,

until soon . . .

he was **enormous!**

Having an enormous dinosaur in the house can be **a bit** tricky.

CRASH!

BUMP!

So we play outside as much as possible.

Dino's favorite game is

"FETCH!"

though he doesn't always bring the ball back.

Making new friends at the park is
also a challenge. Dino's roaring for joy
can sometimes be misunderstood.

All the excitement of being outdoors
makes Dino hungry . . .

and not just for food.

GURGLE!

So we have to keep a close eye on him
if his tummy starts to rumble.

Dino does make an excellent guard dog, though,
because he isn't scared of anything.

BEWARE

Well, **almost** anything!

Sometimes it's hard to get him
to put away his toys at the end of the day.

And bath time makes him sleepy . . .

ZZZZZ

so then it's time for bed.

We thought it was tricky
having *one* dinosaur in the house,
but then we found three more eggs
in our backyard!

So we got a **bigger** house!